I'M A PIG

Keep reading,
singing, & shining
Love, Lori Lynn

1-18-22

Written by
Lori Lynn
of Overall Buddies

Illustrated by
Emily Baum

Dedicated to my sons, Paul and Michael
for all the times we sang this, and other songs
at the top of our lungs
in The Toy and Mazzie
I ♥ U

Special shout outs to the generous sponsors who support my
School & Library Artist Visits, my Kickstarter backers, my pre
order VIPs, my friends, family, followers, & subscribers, and
all of you who continue to champion and encourage my efforts
to serve children, families, and teachers.
I love and appreciate you all!

This book gives back to the community. A portion of all books
sold will be donated to the Overall Buddies non-profit partner,
Children's Square, USA, who care for children & families in
need. Find out more about them and how you might support
their efforts here: childrenssquare.org

I'M A PIG Based on the original song by Lori Lynn Ahrends, ©1992

OVERALL BUDDIES books are available from your favorite bookseller or from www.overallbuddies.com
For information address Overall Buddies PO Box 1054 Council Bluffs, IA 51502, or use the contact page on the website.
Cover and Layout Design: Rachel Thomaier
Printed in the USA by Perfection Press, Logan, Iowa

Publisher's Cataloging-in-Publication data

Names: Ahrends, Lori Lynn, 1961- author. | Baum, Emily, illustrator.
Title: I'm a pig / written by Lori Lynn of Overall Buddies; illustrated by Emily Baum.
Description: Council Bluffs, IA: Overall Buddies, 2022. | Summary: Chronicles a day that a girl is followed around by a cute and cheerful pig. Readers can play "Where's OB" in the pictures.
Identifiers: LCCN: 2021949117 | ISBN: 979-8-9851244-2-2 (hardcover) | 979-8-9851244-0-8 (hardcover)
979-8-9851244-3-9 (paperback) | 979-8-9851244-1-5 (ebook)
Subjects: LCSH Pigs—Juvenile fiction. | Domestic animals—Juvenile fiction. | Stories in rhyme. | CYAC Pigs—Fiction.
Domestic animals—Fiction. | BISAC JUVENILE FICTION / Animals / Pigs | JUVENILE FICTION / Humorous Stories
Classification: LCC PZ7.1. L958 Im 2022 | DDC [E]—dc23

10 9 8 7 6 5 4 3 2 1

I woke up one morning to a **BRIGHT** and **SUNNY** day.

There was a **PIG**
sitting on my bed,

2

and this is what
he had to say,

RIGHT AWAY!

"I'm a **PIG,** I'm a **PIG,** and I'm happy that I'm such!

Thank you very much,
I'm a **PIG!**"

"I'm a **PIG,** I'm a **PIG,**

and I'm happy that I'm such!

Thank you very much, I'm a **PIG!**"

La La

La

La

La La

La La

La

"I'm a **PIG!**"

Br bb   Br bb

Br bb   Br bb

Br bb   Br bb   Br

I went to the

GROCERY STORE

to get some

MILK and BREAD.

When from out behind
the cracker Jacks,

the **PIG** stuck out his head.

And

he

said,

"I'm a **PIG,** I'm a **PIG,** and I'm happy that I'm such! Thank you very much, I'm a **PIG!**"

La

La La

La

La La La La

"I'm a **PIG!**"

Br bb
Br bb
Br bb
Br bb

Br bb
Br bb
Br

I went to school
that day, to
learn
my

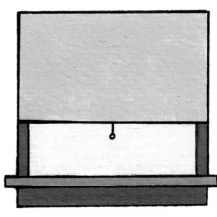

A
B
Cs.

14

The **PIG** snuck in at snack time, and stole my piece of **CHEESE.**

"I'm a **PIG,** I'm a **PIG,** and I'm happy that I'm such!

Thank you very much, I'm a **PIG!**"

16

"I'm a **PIG,** I'm a **PIG,** and I'm happy that I'm such! Thank you very much, I'm a **PIG!**"

La La La La La La La La La

I went to the football game,

to cheer on my home team.

There was the **PIG** in a cheerleading skirt, letting out a scream...

Ready? GO!

"I'm a **PIG,** I'm a **PIG,**

and I'm happy that I'm such!

Rah!

Thank you very much,

Rah! I'm a **PIG!**" Rah!

"I'm a **PIG,** I'm a **PIG,** and I'm happy that I'm such!

Rah!

Thank you very much, **PIG!**"

Rah! I'm a **PIG!** Rah!

I'm a **PIG!**

Rah! Rah!

Br bb   Br bb

Br bb   Br bb

Br bb   Br bb

Br

24

Well, I don't know
where he came from,

I don't know where he's gone.

But I know as long as I live
I'll sing his happy song!

SING ALONG!

"I'm a **PIG,** I'm a **PIG,** and I'm happy that I'm such.

Thank you very much,

I'm a **PIG!"**

"I'm a **PIG,** I'm a **PIG,**
and I'm happy that I'm such!

Thank you
very much,
I'm a
PIG!"

La la la la
La la la la

28

"I'm a **PIG!**"

"I'm a **PIG!**"

"I'm a **PIG!**"

"I'm a **PIG!**"

Lori Lynn Ahrends believes in children and the adults who love and care for them. She is an award winning children's singer songwriter, author, international speaker, and early childhood national trainer. She created the brand, Overall Buddies after 30 years of teaching & training in the early childhood profession. Lori Lynn lives in beautiful Iowa with her perfect little peanut pup, Winston, and her little lion kitty, Simba. She has two wonderful grown sons with lovely wives, and is GiGi to her first blessed grandson. If you want to see what Lori Lynn and her team are up to next, follow Overall Buddies on FB, IG, and YouTube, and check out their website at overallbuddies.com. (photo credit: Julian Adair)

Emily Baum was born and raised in Omaha, Nebraska to a very artistic and creative family. Drawing, painting, and creating has been an obsession ever since she could hold a crayon. Always wanting to learn new skills she has added crochet, sewing, and needle felting to her arsenal. Most days you can find her with several projects to work on. Now a recent resident to Colorado she enjoys hiking with her family or exploring new places with her husband, two daughters, and two naughty, but lovable pups.

Rachel Thomaier is a passionate graphic designer who is a problem solver, trend setter, and strategic thinker. Her multiple awards include a 2017 Nebraska Book Award, a gold ADDY award, and a silver ADDY award. Rachel grew up in Grand Island, Nebraska, where she always had a love for all things design. She graduated with honors from the University of Nebraska at Kearney with a Bachelor of Fine Arts in Visual Communication and Design. Rachel currently lives in Omaha, Nebraska. In her spare time she likes to challenge herself with learning new and upcoming aspects of design. She also enjoys spending time with her husband, Cory, and their dog, Duchess. Learn more at rachelsmdesigns.com.

Hi! I'm OB! I'm hiding in most of the pictures of this book! How many times can you find me?

Order your very own OB plush toy at overallbuddies.com!

Let's stay connected! Reach out to us and share pictures or quotes from your child about the *I'm A Pig* book by posting on Facebook and/or Instagram. Use the hashtag #overallbuddies on your posts so we can find one another!

Thanks for being our reading & singing buddy!